DISCARD

DISCARD

DISCARD

Me Too!

Valeri Gorbachev

Holiday House / New York

"I love snow!" said Bear.
"Me too!" said Chipmunk.

"I will dig," said Bear.
"Me too!" said Chipmunk.

"I will make a snowman,"
said Bear.
"Me too!" said Chipmunk.

"I want to skate," said Bear.
"Me too!" said Chipmunk.

"I fell!" said Bear.
"Me too!" said Chipmunk.

"I love to ski!" said Bear.
"Me too!" said Chipmunk.

"The snow is deep," said Bear.
"It is up to my knees."
"Mine too!" said Chipmunk.

"Let's go home," said Bear.
"I am cold."
"Me too!" said Chipmunk.

"I had fun in the snow,"
said Bear.

"Me too!" said Chipmunk.

"Sweet dreams," said Bear.

"You too!" said Chipmunk.

Copyright © 2013 by Valeri Gorbachev
All Rights Reserved
HOLIDAY HOUSE is registered in the U.S. Patent and Trademark Office.
Printed and Bound in April 2013 at Tien Wah Press, Johor Bahru, Johor, Malaysia.
The text typeface is Report School Regular.
The artwork was created with watercolor and ink.
www.holidayhouse.com
First Edition
1 3 5 7 9 10 8 6 4 2

Library of Congress Cataloging-in-Publication Data
Gorbachev, Valeri.
Me too! / by Valeri Gorbachev. — 1st ed.
p. cm. — (I like to read)
Summary: "Chipmunk and Bear spend a snowy day together and
discover that they like to do all of the same things."
— Provided by publisher.
ISBN 978-0-8234-2744-4 (hardcover)
[1. Snow—Fiction. 2. Chipmunks—Fiction. 3. Bears—Fiction.] I. Title.
PZ7.G6475Me 2013
[E]—dc23
2012039294

I Like to Read® Books
You will like all of them!

Boy, Bird, and Dog by David McPhail

Car Goes Far by Michael Garland

Come Back, Ben by John Hassett and Ann Hassett

Dinosaurs Don't, Dinosaurs Do by Steve Björkman

Fireman Fred by Lynn Rowe Reed

Fish Had a Wish by Michael Garland

The Fly Flew In by David Catrow

Happy Cat by Steve Henry

I Have a Garden by Bob Barner

I Will Try by Marilyn Janovitz

Late Nate in a Race by Emily Arnold McCully

The Lion and the Mice
by Rebecca Emberley and Ed Emberley

Look! by Ted Lewin

Me Too! by Valeri Gorbachev

Mice on Ice
by Rebecca Emberley and Ed Emberley

Pete Won't Eat by Emily Arnold McCully

Pig Has a Plan by Ethan Long

Sam and the Big Kids by Emily Arnold McCully

See Me Dig by Paul Meisel

See Me Run by Paul Meisel
A THEODOR SEUSS GEISEL AWARD HONOR BOOK

Sick Day by David McPhail

What Am I? Where Am I? by Ted Lewin

You Can Do It! by Betsy Lewin

Visit holidayhouse.com to read more
about I Like to Read® Books.